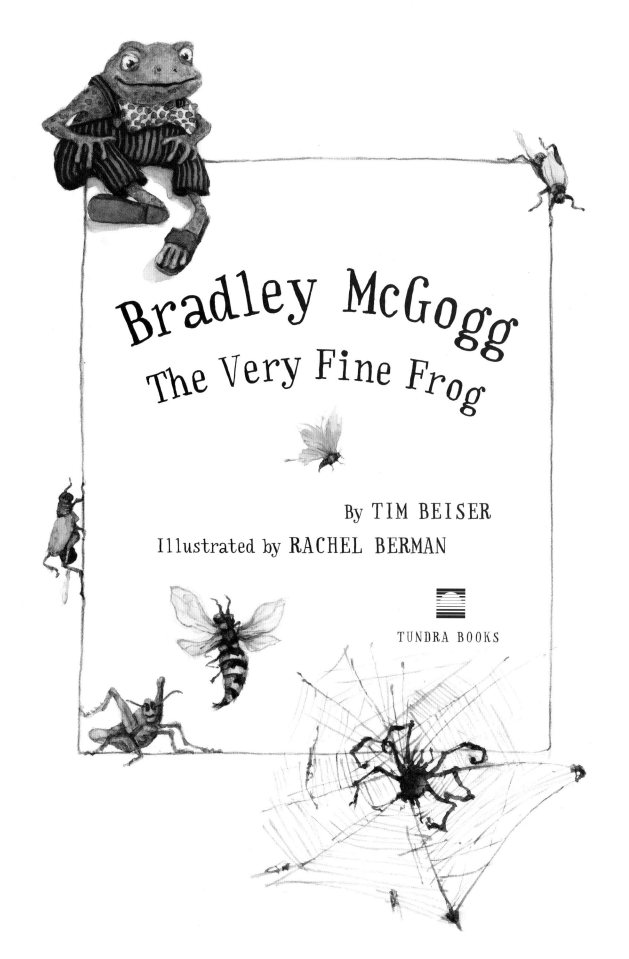

Bradley McGogg
The Very Fine Frog

By TIM BEISER

Illustrated by RACHEL BERMAN

TUNDRA BOOKS

Published in Canada by Tundra Books,
75 Sherbourne Street, Toronto, Ontario M5A 2P9

Published in the United States by Tundra Books of Northern New York,
P.O. Box 1030, Plattsburgh, New York 12901

Library of Congress Control Number: 2008903003

LIBRARY AND ARCHIVES CANADA CATALOGUING IN PUBLICATION

Beiser, Tim, 1959-
Bradley McGogg, the very fine frog / Tim Beiser ; illustrator: Rachel Berman.
Target audience: For ages 2-5.

ISBN 978-0-88776-864-4

1. Frogs–Juvenile fiction. 2. Picture books for children.
I. Berman, Rachel, 1947- II. Title.

PS8603.E42846B73 2009   jC813'.6   C2008-902059-6

We acknowledge the financial support of the Government of Canada through the Book Publishing Industry
Development Program (BPIDP) and that of the Government of Ontario through the Ontario Media Development
Corporation's Ontario Book Initiative. We further acknowledge the support of the Canada Council for the Arts
and the Ontario Arts Council for our publishing program.

ONTARIO ARTS COUNCIL
CONSEIL DES ARTS DE L'ONTARIO

Cover illustration by Rachel Berman • Design by CS Richardson

Printed and bound in China
Medium: Watercolor and gouache on rag

1 2 3 4 5 6   14 13 12 11 10 09

Katie McGuire,

When you were in the first
grade, you asked me to write you
a story about a frog. So I did.
And that is why this book is
dedicated to you.

　　　　　　— Uncle Tim

To M.O.M.H.

　　　　　　— RB

Bradley McGogg was a very fine frog
who happily napped in a hollowed-out log.

This log in a bog, where our frog spent his days,
was a pad Brad had had since his pollywog phase.

"Oh, beautiful bog," croaked McGogg.
"What an Eden!
You're filled to the gills with
good frog things to feed on!"

Said Bradley McGogg on one hot summer day,
"I'm needing a feeding. I'm wasting away!"

So up in his cupboard,
Brad grabbed for some luncheon.
But what a surprise!
He found nothing to munch on.

"There's nothing to eat here!"
exclaimed the poor frog.
"What happened to all of the
food in my log?"

Brad sat on a stump,
    and he pondered and pondered.
      He strained his frog brain,
        but his mind kind of wandered.

Pretty soon (around noon), Bradley had a clear vision.
He knew what to do. He had made a decision!

"My gosh, I'm awash with new neighbors to meet.
My task is to ask them to share what they eat!"

Hop, hop! His first stop was to visit Miss Mouse
in the underhill nest that she used for a house.

"Miss Mousie," he said, "may I trouble to borrow
some grubs for my supper? I'll pay you tomorrow."

She squeaked very meekly, "Come in if you please"
and made him a snack of rye crackers and cheese.

With his tiny green fingers
he stifled a gasp,
in fright at the sight
of the cheese in her grasp.

Cheddar with chives and a
peppercorn dusting!
He had never seen anything
quite so disgusting.

Said the frog to the mouse,
who insisted he try it,
"Drat the lot! I forgot —
I just started a diet!"

Hop, hop! His next stop was to call on the bear
who lived in a den that he shared with a hare.

"Herr Bear and Herr Hare, I arrive half alive,
and ask for a sweet, buzzy snack from your hive!"

At a spot near their grotto,
  the bear and the bunny
    presented Brad carrots
      all covered in honey.

Eww! What is that? Such horrible stew!
Orange-colored roots that are sticky with goo!

That was his thought —
    he of course didn't share it.
      So as not to be rude,
          Bradley reached for one carrot.

"What a treat!" said the frog.
"Home it goes in my bucket."
(Instead, Bradley fled
to a mole hole to chuck it.)

Hop, hop! His next stop was the cow on the slope, whose mooing and chewing gave Bradley great hope.

But he stopped in mid-hop
    when he caught Miss Moo grazing.
What she chewed for her food
    Bradley found quite amazing.

She was munching on clover
    and snacking on grass!
To avoid the same lunch,
    Bradley gave her a pass.

So sadly did Bradley slog back to his bog
to mope without hope for some food in his log.

But when he got home, Bradley croaked with elation.
His hall was a-crawl with a pest infestation.

Mmm, bugs are tasty! *Mmm*, bugs, delicious!
Bugs are a bog frog's most favorite dishes!

He sat down to dinner and feasted on pails
of maggots, mosquitoes, grasshoppers, and snails.

He gobbled up stinkbugs and sweet, buzzy bees,
flies, squirmy worms, crunchy roaches, and fleas.

Brad said, as he fed
    on some dragonfly wings:
        "Holy smokes! Other folks
            eat some pretty strange things."

The End.